MIR★CLES

First published 2023

Copyright © Marguerite Coutinho 2023

The right of Marguerite Coutinho to be identified as the author of this work has been asserted in accordance with the Copyright, Designs & Patents Act 1988.

All rights reserved. No part of this book may be reproduced, stored in a retrieval system, or transmitted in any form or by any means, electronic, electrostatic, magnetic tape, mechanical, photocopying, recording or otherwise, without the written permission of the copyright holder.

Published under licence by Brown Dog Books and
The Self-Publishing Partnership Ltd, 10b Greenway Farm, Bath Rd,
Wick, nr. Bath BS30 5RL

www.selfpublishingpartnership.co.uk

ISBN printed book: 978-1-83952-660-2

Cover design by Kevin Rylands
Internal design by Andrew Easton

Printed and bound by CPI Group (UK) Ltd, Croydon, CR0 4YY

This book is printed on FSC® certified paper

Foreword

When I came to terms with the realisation that the time for me to take on the role of a writer had finally arrived, I found myself wondering what subject I should write about.

Ever since I was a child, I have always loved reading and I spent most of my pocket money on books. I admired writers like Enid Blyton tremendously and saved money each Christmas to buy the Bunty Annuals. I thought it would be fun to write children's books and vowed that I would do so once I retired.

Having made up my mind to write, I was stumped with finding a suitable idea and prayed for inspiration. Then, out of the blue, it hit me! – I would reinvent the four miracles in the Gospels involving children by bringing their characters to life and giving them suitable family backgrounds. However, as there were only four recorded miracles I decided to create the fifth who would be the nephew of the bridegroom whose wedding Jesus attended.

So, these stories are historical events that took place, but told through the eyes of five different children who all seem to see Jesus in the same way.

I want to extend my most sincere appreciation to Nympha, who helped me with the Epilogue, and to Alan and Ursula for pointing out my errors to me, and to all my other friends who commended the manuscript.

Finally, I want to show my deepest gratitude to God without Whose inspiration this book would never have been written at all.

'But Jesus said, "Suffer little children, and forbid them not, to come unto me; for such is the kingdom of heaven."'
(Matthew 19:14)

Contents

1. The Wedding Feast at Cana — Page 11

2. Jairus's Daughter — Page 22

3. Five Loaves and Two Fish — Page 31

4. Jesus Heals a Boy — Page 43

5. The Syro-Phoenician Girl — Page 51

1.
The Wedding Feast at Cana

A golden ray of sunlight streamed through the shutters of the windows in my little room and touched my eyes with a gentle kiss. I opened them and flew excitedly to the window, throwing aside the shutters to gaze in great expectation at the scene below.

Mother was out in the yard with Anna, my elder sister, putting the finishing touches to the shelter, or 'chuppah', which was elaborately embellished with trellises of creeping vine and a canopy or covering made up of a sparkling white sheet. I drew in my breath in admiration. It looked amazing!

I quickly splashed cold water on my face, changed my clothes and ran down the stairs into the garden to join Mother and Anna. As soon as I got there, Mother assigned me with a series of unnecessary tasks – or so I thought. Later, I was to realise how important they were to be.

I rushed into the kitchen from where a most savoury aroma of cooking meat mixed with spices was floating out into the bright sunshine. I came to a halt and greedily eyed with delight all the delicious food that was being prepared in that small but incredibly industrious space. There were bowls of olives and dates, fruit of every kind that I could think of, and a pot of lamb stew bubbling in a huge cauldron on the blazing fire with chickens as far as the eye could see roasting on the spit. The cornucopia of smells floating in the air hit me so hard that I started to dribble.

'Well, Mathieu, I'm glad you've finally decided to get up and join us,' I could not mistake the cheery, lilting voice of my grandmother. 'Sit down and have something to eat.'

An extremely beautiful lady dressed in clean white linen with a cord of twisted yarn encircling her waist placed a plate of flatbread and a cup of milk on the table in front of me. I looked up at her and smiled, 'Thank you.'

She wasn't very old (not as old as my grandmother), perhaps in her late forties, but what struck me about her was her serenity and calmness in all that hustle and bustle of the wedding kitchen. Strangely enough, my grandmother was also calm and so were all the cooks and servants. They were going about their duties in a purposeful manner, moving quickly but methodically. Sitting there and having my breakfast, I realised that the beautiful lady was giving the orders and that she was in control. Who *was* she?

'I just came to see if everything is alright,' *Ammo* Benjamin could not hide the inflection of anxiety and worry in his voice.

My grandmother immediately shooed him out of the kitchen. 'Everything is going just splendidly, with your *Atu* Mary doing a wonderful job here. Go out and relax, Benjamin, and get ready for your big day! You have to look your best. So stop worrying and leave all the work to us. For once!'

Breathing out a great sigh of relief at the glorious spectacle of food all around him, my uncle turned and went away.

'Mother asked me to tell you, *Savta*,' I said to my grandmother, 'not to forget to fill all the stone jars with water for the foot washing of our guests.'

'Huh!' my grandmother scoffed. 'As if I could forget that! It is such an important part of our tradition.'

I shot out of the overheated kitchen and skipped to the front of the house to look for my father whose task was to remind the Master of Ceremonies to have the wine poured into jugs with goblets arranged on trays, to serve the guests on a separate table, so that the servants could simply pick them up and carry them out into the garden during the celebration.

'That's a great idea,' he said. My father, Simon, the bridegroom's brother was a very kind and gentle man. I loved him dearly.

'I will do just that. Hurry up and get ready, Mathieu. You're not yet dressed, are you?' He patted my head and I could hear him laughing as I dashed back into the house to change for my uncle Benjamin's wedding.

From my bedroom window I spotted some of the first guests appearing like dots on the horizon. As I watched intently, the dots grew bigger and bigger and bigger in the shimmering heat. Then, like a vision in a mirage, they turned into a crowd of people – men, women and children (mostly men) – walking in an unhurried yet purposeful manner towards our humble home. Their footsteps conjured up clouds of dust, and as they approached the entrance I noticed an extremely good-looking young man of about 30 years leading in the front row of the crowd. I leaned over to get a closer look and almost toppled out of the window!

MIRACLES

MIRACLES

I lunged backwards to prevent myself from falling over and scuttled down the stone steps to the yard for the second time that morning. I ran towards the crowd, eager to be in the thick of things, when my attention was caught again by the appearance of the young man.

He was tall and well-built, but that wasn't what enthralled me. It was the way he carried himself, so poised and sedate even after that long, dusty walk. He looked regal, majestic even. I watched fascinated, my eyes transfixed on his face as he marched up to our house. He stood out from the midst of the crowd, set apart, unique. The curls of his shoulder-length black hair bounced to the rhythm of his stride. I continued to stare unashamedly, and as he passed by me he broke out into a smile. It was like the sun rising over the horizon; it spread out across his entire face to his beautiful brown eyes, which danced in merriment. My heart skipped a beat! I felt a warm glow of love because of the way he looked at me. Who *was* he?

'*Shlama L'oux!* Peace be with you!' said my grandfather, bowing low before the young man. 'Welcome! Welcome!' He continued to bow low to the crowd streaming into our garden.

Suddenly, a cacophony of sounds rent the air. The clamour of people talking, laughing, crying and shouting all at once seemed to shatter the tranquillity of the morning's quiet activities. They were all given light refreshments of fruit and water or fresh juice to quench their thirst after the heat of the long journey.

Then the wedding ceremony began.

A Jewish wedding ceremony – *'nisuin'* follows Jewish laws and traditions. My uncle Benjamin entered the *'chuppah'* (symbolic of Abraham's tent open to hospitality) first, which represented his ownership of the home. Then Rhoda, his bride went in with a veil covering her face, head and shoulders. The bridal couple were married under the *'chuppah'*. The Rabbi blessed them, and my uncle and Rhoda placed a ring on each other's finger. Blessings were recited by their family members and the Rabbi. Then my uncle broke the glass and everyone shouted *'Mazel Tovi!* meaning 'Congratulations!'

Then once again the magnanimity and dignity of the sedate occasion erupted into an uproar of shouts of encouragement to the newlyweds, with the sounds of chatter, laughter and singing to music playing in the background. The younger guests milled around, while the older, elderly and more mature ones found places to sit down and chat quietly about the wedding. The *'chuppah'* was transformed into an arbour for the bridal couple and soon drinks and food were being served on trays and large platters.

I watched the people for a while as my eager eyes scanned the crowd for sightings of my new hero. He was sitting among the younger guests who were talking, laughing merrily and drinking the wine that was flowing freely among the crowd. He was listening intently to them and occasionally threw his head back to laugh along with his friends. I gazed at him in admiration.

'If you open your mouth any bigger, ten flies will get into it. What are you staring at anyway?' It was Anna, my sister, who had brought me some food. I didn't realise that my mouth was open and quickly shut it with a snap.

'Are you coming to play with us, or are you going to sit there gawping at the crowd?' I could hear the sound of disdain and mockery in her voice.

'I'll join you as soon as I have my lunch,' I said sheepishly.

I gobbled my food in a hurry and soon scampered off to the other side of the house to play with my sister and my friends. We must have been there for more than an hour when we heard music playing and people cheering. It was the special dance of the bridal couple.

We raced back to the house to watch them, mesmerised as they moved in tandem with each other. That is what marriage is supposed to be, isn't it? Two people moving and living in sync with each other. Then, as they bowed gracefully to a tumultuous applause, the tempo of the music changed and took on a livelier beat. The young man and his friends sprinted onto the dancefloor and soon they were twirling and leaping about, having the time of their lives.

As the sun started to set it splashed a splatter of colours across the sky – red, orange, purple and pink. The servants began to light up the *'chuppah'* and brought lamps and tapers to the tables. In the candlelight I saw the beautiful lady, Mary, and my grandmother conversing in low voices. Grandmother looked very serious and worried. Mary put a comforting arm around Grandmother's shoulders and smiled reassuringly at her. Then she swiftly glided straight towards the young man, who was now standing aside and wiping his face with a large linen handkerchief. He smiled lovingly at her as she approached him.

'They have no wine,' she said. It was not a request, just a simple statement of fact.

'Woman, what is that to me?' he asked. I gasped at his audacity. 'My time has not yet come.'

MIRACLES

What *did* he mean? It sounded so strange.

'That's Yeshua's mother,' said my friend, Rueben who had come out to look for me. 'They are from Nazareth. Their family are carpenters.'

'How do you know this?' I glared indignantly at Rueben.

Rueben shrugged. 'I heard them talking in the kitchen. You've run out of wine!'

My heart sank in dismay! Then I broke out in a cold sweat. Running out of wine was a serious thing. It would cause abject humiliation to our family, and Uncle Benjamin would be in disgrace. He would never live it down.

Just then I spotted Yeshua moving determinedly in the direction of the kitchen. I followed him with Rueben hot on my heels.

'Do whatever he tells you.' I was just in time to hear Mary speaking confidently to the servants.

Yeshua looked, with a mixture of interest and delight, all around the bustling bursting kitchen. He seemed so relaxed, not at all in a hurry to help. What was he going to do? What did Mary expect him to do?

My eager eyes searched his face as he stood staring for some time at the large stone containers that I had told my grandmother to fill up with water for the guests to wash with. They were all empty now.

'Fill those jars with water to the brim,' he said authoritatively.

While the servants hastened to do his bidding, Rueben plucked at my sleeve and we both retired to a discreet corner of the kitchen to watch the proceedings, which we both thought were going to be very interesting indeed.

When all the jars were filled with water, Yeshua stood straight and tall. He looked up at the rafters and spread his arms wide in an attitude of praise. His eyes were shut as he murmured a prayer. Then he told the Chief Steward to fill a jug with the water from one of the stone jars and to drink it.

The Chief Steward did as he was told. He poured the water from the jug into a bronze goblet and drank. He licked his lips in delight and stared at Yeshua, his eyes as large as saucers.

'This is the best wine I have ever tasted in my entire life!' he exclaimed in surprise. 'It is so sweet, so fruity, so delicious! It's incredible! I love it!' He made a little wave with his left hand every time he spoke, bouncing up and down simultaneously.

Rueben and I rushed towards the stone jars and looked into the sparkling crystal-clear water. Our own reflections stared back at us. We exchanged glances – we both had the same idea. We each grabbed a clay cup from the shelves above the jars, dipped them into the water and drank. We did precisely what the Chief Steward did: licked our lips, wiped the back of our hands against our mouths and promptly drained the contents of the cup. Then we laughed with excitement and sheer joy and had another draught.

'Steady on there, lads!' Yeshua laughed. 'We don't want you getting drunk at such a young age, now, do we?!' We shook our heads in embarrassment.

The Chief Steward give a glass of wine to the Master of Ceremonies, who savoured the draught in his mouth and then reacted with incredulity to the taste.

'Mmmm,' he sighed, nodding appreciatively. 'This wine is absolutely splendid! People usually serve the best wine first, but you

– you have kept it till the end,' he added to my grandfather who was standing next to my grandmother with Mary by her side. 'Very clever, eh!' He guffawed, slapping my grandfather in a camaraderie manner on his back that sent him spluttering.

Across the room, I saw Yeshua look at his mother who mouthed, 'Thank you' to him. He smiled, inclining his head ever so slightly in gracious acknowledgment. My heart warmed at the sight, and I thought, what a lovely close relationship they had with one another.

Rueben and I looked at each other in amazement. I found myself wondering, who *is* he and *how* did he do it? How did he change water into wine like that? It was nothing short of a miracle. I spent a while marvelling at it all. It was not until another exciting and dramatic miracle happened a few months later that I began to fit the pieces of the puzzle together.

MIRACLES

2.
Jairus's Daughter

'Naomi, come quickly! It's David. He has come to see you.' My mother came into the room looking eager and excited. 'What are you doing, child? Don't keep him waiting.'

I got up and smiled dreamily at my mother. Then hurriedly donning my headscarf, I glided out of the room to meet my beloved betrothed.

David was the handsomest, most wonderful and most eligible bachelor in all of Judea and he was going to marry me. Yet, this betrothal may never have come to pass if the most extraordinary miracle had never happened to me three years ago.

I woke up one morning with a splitting headache. My mouth felt dry and my joints ached. My whole body was wracked with pain from the crown of my head to the soles of my feet. I didn't need a rocket scientist to tell me that I was very ill indeed.

My mother panicked when she saw me. I looked a mess: hair

straggled all over my tiny face; eyes as large as saucers, glazed and staring into space like a zombie.

'What is wrong, my darling child? Are you ill?' she asked, screwing up her face in concern. 'You look as pale as a ghost.'

She stretched out her hand and touched my forehead.

'Ahhhh!' she shrieked. 'You are burning up! I must tell your father.' And off she went to look for my poor father, calling out to him, flustered and distracted.

'Jairus, Jairus! You must come and see. Naomi is very ill.' The desperation and fear in her voice could not be contained.

My father came rushing out of his room, took one look at me and put his hands to his head. I was afraid he was going to tear his hair out! He was so distraught!

'I'm sure it's nothing very serious that can't be cured with a little medicine, Father,' I said placatingly.

'We shall see,' my mother answered. Her face was like flint. 'Get back into bed and stay there. You're not coming out until the fever drops. And that's that, young lady!'

I skittered back to my room, but as my mother tucked me in, I could see my father now holding his face in his hands. Surely he didn't think I was going to die!

A few minutes later, my nursemaid brought me a warm drink in a clay cup. I drank it all down to the very last sip as it was really delicious. Then I lay back and fell asleep

MIRACLES

My father was the ruler of the synagogue. He was well-respected and known to be an honourable man in the community. Everybody loved him. I was his only child. So it was no surprise that both my parents were so concerned about my welfare. I meant everything to them.

I must have slept for about three hours because it was noon when I woke up again. The drink the nurse gave me must have had a sleeping potion in it. Unfortunately, it didn't cure me of my ailment. I felt groggy and my body was hot with the fever.

'*Ima.*' I tried to call my mother but it came out as a croak. Now to make matters worse I had a frog in my throat. I cleared my throat and called again. This time my voice was louder. '*Ima*, please come!'

The nursemaid heard me and ran joyfully into the room, but when she saw my haggard eyes and touched my burning face, her smile vanished and her joy turned to sorrow.

'She's got the fever!' she wailed.

My parents rushed into the room. They stared at me, then looked at each other in consternation.

'What are we going to *do*?' my mother howled hysterically.

'The Healer is in town today,' said one of the servants who was standing in the doorway to my room. 'You can ask him to come and heal *thalitha*.'

My father nodded. 'You are right. The Rabbi is the only one who can heal Naomi. We must go at once. Come!'

And they both set off to look for the Rabbi.

MIRACLES

The crowded street was heaving with people who had come to see the Teacher and be healed. Everyone wanted a piece of the pie – a miracle from the Miracle Worker. Yeshua was like a celebrity of his day. Children ran after him to touch him or hold his hand; toddlers held up their chubby arms, begging him to lift them up and be tossed into the air, gurgling with laughter as he caught them and hugged them close before letting them go squealing in delight to their mothers. They adored him because they knew he loved them too.

Today was like any other day, and like every other village when the Teacher was visiting: crowded and congested. My father got to Yeshua just as he turned the corner into the market place where the people were waiting for him.

He flung himself at Yeshua's feet and pleaded, 'Master, my child is ill. She is dying. Please come and put your hands on her so that she will be healed.'

Yeshua looked down at him, his brown eyes filled with love and compassion. He held out his hands to lift my father up and said kindly, 'Do not be afraid. I will come. Lead the way.'

Almost sick with relief, my father sighed deeply, straightened up and turned towards the direction of our house. Immediately, the crowd that had been waiting for him surged forwards like a tidal wave with the Master swallowed up in the midst of them. They jostled and pushed, heaved and shoved, almost crushing him in their desire to touch him, get near to him or simply to gaze upon his beautiful face.

Suddenly, Yeshua stopped short in his tracks.

'Who touched me?' he asked.

When they all denied it, Peter said reasonably, 'Master, the people

MIRACLES

are crowding and pressing against you. How can you ask "*who touched me?*" You are hemmed in on *every* side. People are touching you in *every* direction.'

Yeshua shook his head, his glossy black curls bouncing off his shoulders.

'Someone touched me,' he insisted. 'I know that power has gone out from me.'

MIRACLES

He swung round to glance behind him just as a woman came trembling towards him to fall at his feet.

'It was I, Master,' she sobbed. 'I have suffered for twelve years from this debilitating disease and I was unclean. I have been shunned and rejected by my family and friends. I have spent everything on doctors and nothing has helped me until … until …'

'You touched the hem of my garment,' Yeshua interrupted her regarding her with great tenderness and compassion.

'Yes,' the woman smiled up at him, her face radiant through her tears, like the sun appearing from behind a rain cloud. 'And I am healed!' She could not contain her joy and threw her hands up in praise to God. 'Thank you! Thank you so much!' she cried.

Then, just as he did my father, Yeshua held out his hands and drew her to her feet. He said to her, 'Daughter, your faith has healed you. Go in peace and be freed from your suffering.'

While Yeshua was still speaking, one of the servants came to my father. 'Your daughter is dead,' he said. 'Do not trouble the Teacher anymore.'

My father let out a little groan of anguish and clutched his head in his hands. 'Oh no! What am I going to do! She's just a child, only twelve years old!' he cried, looking piteously at Yeshua.

Hearing this, the Master placed his hand on my father's shoulder and said reassuringly to him, 'Do not be afraid; just believe, and she will be healed.' Then Yeshua gestured for my father to lead the way.

When they arrived at our house, the Rabbi did not allow anyone to go in with him except for Peter, James and John, and my father and mother, of course. The house was packed to capacity with people wailing and mourning for me.

'Stop wailing,' Yeshua said. 'She is not dead, but asleep.'

They laughed at him and mocked him, knowing full well that I was dead.

Yeshua ignored them and calmly approached the bed on which I lay.

As I slept the second time, I had the most wonderful dream. I dreamt I was in a very beautiful garden that had a plethora of flora and trees, with fields of wild flowers and bright green grass beyond, stretching as far as the eye could see. I was wearing a pure white linen gown with a wreath of large white daisies on my head. My long silky black hair flowed in the breeze, while exotic birds chirped and tweeted merrily and melodiously in the trees.

Then, in the distance, I saw a figure all clad in white appear apparently out of nowhere and begin to walk slowly towards me. I ran forwards, and as I approached the figure, I noticed that a brilliant radiance of light seemed to emanate from him, spreading an iridescent glow through the whole landscape. I looked up into the most dazzling and beautiful face I had ever seen in my entire life. His brown eyes were gentle and kind. I fell at his feet in awe at the splendour of his appearance. He held out his right hand and when I placed mine in his, he raised me up and said, *'Talitha kumi!'*

Immediately, I awoke from my dream. My spirit returned and I stood up.

Everyone gasped in amazement. My parents were overjoyed and

MIRACLES

bowed before the Master, thanking him profusely, laughing and crying at the same time.

'Give her something to eat,' Yeshua said to them, smiling indulgently at their happiness. 'And do not tell anyone about what has happened here today.'

Then he left.

3.
Five Loaves and Two Fish

I rose at the crack of dawn. I just couldn't sleep. I was too excited. I had heard that Yeshua was coming to Bethsaida and I was determined to see him. I had heard that he was a very good teacher, that he healed the sick, lame and blind, and that he loved children. I wanted to listen to his teaching and I longed for him to bless me like he did the others.

The large yellow orb of the sun peered over the horizon like a bridegroom coming out of his bedchamber. It cast its golden rays across the sky, chasing away the blackness of the night and transforming the heavens into a riot of colours – red, orange and yellow – as it slowly rose higher and higher as the day got brighter and brighter.

I knew it was time to get up. I splashed cold water on my face and changed my clothes before you could say 'Jack Robinson!' Then I raced down the stairs to the kitchen where I found my mother preparing breakfast.

She looked at me in surprise. 'You're up early, Samuel,' she said. 'Couldn't sleep?'

I hung my head. 'No. I am so excited, *Ima*!'

'Why am I not surprised?' my mother exclaimed. 'You've been

longing to see the Teacher for a long, long time, haven't you?' She set a breakfast of warm freshly made unleavened bread and milk on the table before me.

'Yes,' I replied sheepishly.

'I've got you some bread and fish with a flagon of water for your lunch. You're bound to get hungry with all that walking. Make sure you get home before sunset, will you? Don't even think about playing on the way back.'

'Of course I won't, *Ima*,' I said meekly. 'And thank you for the lunch.'

'Finish your breakfast and run along. The others will be waiting for you.'

I grabbed the basket with my lunch in it, and kissed my mother goodbye. Then I raced to the end of the road where I would be joining my friend, Nathan, and his father. My father and two older brothers had work to do in the fields, so they couldn't come along with us.

As we walked along the long and dusty road to the shores of the Sea of Galilee, I heard some extremely interesting stories about Yeshua and what he had been doing in Gennesareth.

'Did you hear that he brought Jairus's daughter back from the dead?' Nathan asked me as we trudged along the path, kicking up little clouds of dust and scattering stones with our heels.

'Nooo!' I replied. 'I never knew about that.'

Nathan puffed himself up with pride and importance, and in a rather pompous manner, he went on to tell me the story. 'Yeah, she was quite dead, wasn't she? As dead as a doorpost!' he said dramatically. 'But the Rabbi restored her to life and Jairus was overjoyed.'

MIRACLES

'But that's not all,' Nathan's father said. 'He also healed a woman on the way.'

'Really?' I asked, torn between curiosity, excitement and the fear of missing out. Why do I never hear anything exciting first?!

'Do you want to know how he did it?' Nathan cut in. And before his father could say anything else, he added, almost beside himself with excitement. 'She simply touched the hem of his garment and she was healed.'

'Wow! That's awesome!' I exclaimed. 'How wonderful for the woman! She must have been so grateful.'

'She was,' agreed Nathan's father, nodding. 'Yeshua is so awesome! He does so many great miracles. People believe he is the Messiah.'

'Really?' I breathed, incredulous. I thought I was beginning to sound like a broken record. 'What if he is?' I asked. 'Who do *you* think he is?'

Nathan's father sighed deeply. 'I don't know,' he said, thoughtfully stroking his beard. He was quite a rough, stocky man with a heart of gold and I knew that he and his sons, Nathan's older brothers, worked hard on the farm to enjoy a comfortable life. Nathan's mother had died giving birth to him. My mother was kind to them and often sent them food and other gifts as my father and Nathan's father were close friends.

'I have never met him, but I am certainly looking forward to hearing him teach today. They say he is wise beyond his years and speaks like a Rabbi, although he is actually a carpenter by trade,' Nathan's father said.

'Wow!' I could not help myself. Before I could think of something else to say, the exclamation had escaped my lips like a refrain from a song.

MIRACLES

'Well, we shall see and hear him today. Then we can make up our minds whether he is the Messiah or just another clever itinerant preacher,' Nathan's father stated wisely.

We rounded a bend in the road that led to the shores of the Sea of Galilee. We saw a huge crowd of people walking away from the sea towards the hilly area where there were little clumps of trees to provide shade for the travellers as the day got hotter. We followed them and soon found a shady spot near some bushes to rest where we had a vantage view of Yeshua and his friends, who were called his 'disciples'. Apparently, there were twelve of them, but Nathan pointed only six out to me.

The first was Peter, a stocky, buff and loud fisherman, with his brother, Andrew, who was tall and well built. He seemed like a really good sort. Then there were James and John, the sons of Zebedee, who were also fishermen. My jaw dropped as I looked at John – tall, handsome with a curly, unruly mop of hair. He was so young! I do not think that he was more than 18 years old, which would have made him only six years older than me.

'That's Philip,' Nathan's dad said, pointing to another dashing and smiling young man.

Apparently, it was Philip and Andrew who first made contact with the Rabbi. They had been John the Baptiser's disciples, and then had moved on to become Yeshua's first 'chosen ones'. How amazing was that! If only I had been older, I thought, *I* might have been one of them. Little did I know the part I was to play in the Rabbi's life and how far-reaching it would be.

I was jolted out of my reverie by Nathan's loud voice. It was a rude awakening from my sweet daydreams.

'With his friend, Nathaniel, my namesake,' Nathan piped in excitedly. 'I don't know any of the others.'

'I think that's Judas Iscariot, over there,' said his father, indicating a grim, bearded, older man wearing a dark green cloak and black turban.

'He looks like a magician,' Nathan said in a loud whisper. We both giggled.

'That's not funny,' his father, scolded. 'You know you shouldn't be talking about magic. It's against the law.'

'I'm sorry, *Abba*,' Nathan looked downcast, but not for long. 'Is that Yeshua sitting on the rock beside Peter?' he asked his dad.

'I believe it is,' his father answered gravely. 'And I think that's Thomas standing on the other side of Yeshua with Matthew, the tax collector next to him. Look, he is about to speak.'

I looked at Thomas, who was quite rotund and robust, standing beside the rock on which Yeshua was sitting, with his feet slightly apart. Then my eyes darted to Peter on the other side standing in much the same manner with arms akimbo, surveying the crowd. The other disciples were also standing behind Yeshua in a semicircle. It flashed across my mind that they were forming a sort of protective shield around their Master. They looked like his bodyguards. But *what* was it they were protecting him from?

Yeshua opened his mouth to speak and the crowd fell silent. He told us so many parables, about the kingdom of heaven and how we can get there. He spoke with an authority that I had never seen or heard before. Whenever our teachers taught us, we invariably dozed

MIRACLES

off or played around, always getting into trouble. With Yeshua it was different. He was so interesting and his stories were beautifully woven into the fabric of our lives that we were leaning over, listening intently, completely captivated by him. He talked about the trees bearing fruit in the right season and how nature obeyed God; he talked about the seas, rivers and lakes yielding food for our consumption and how God provided everything possible for His children, so we don't have to worry about anything. We were enthralled.

As the afternoon wore on, I suddenly realised that I was feeling very hungry and that my stomach had started to rumble. I peeped into the little basket mother had given me and was disappointed with the sight that met my eyes: five loaves of bread and two grilled fish! Seriously?! I was gutted! I turned red in embarrassment. I couldn't share my lunch with Nathan and his father, and as far as I could see, I didn't think they had brought anything except for their skins of water.

What was I to do? I couldn't eat on my own, all by myself. That wouldn't be polite. In my culture we were always taught to be kind and to share what we had with others.

I sat up when I saw that Yeshua had stopped speaking, and that there was once again the hum of myriads of people talking instead. I could see the disciples gather around Yeshua and wondered what was going on. Yeshua said something to Philip and he threw his arms up in a gesture of despair. What *was* going on?

Then I saw Philip and Andrew walk towards us in a rather purposeful manner while the other disciples mingled with the clusters of people talking to them briefly. Most of the people seemed to be shaking their heads.

MIRACLES

'What's happening?' I asked. 'Is something the matter?' The concern in my voice came out in a croak.

'They are going around asking people if they have any food to eat,' said a young lad who had just come running in our direction. He was about the same age as me and was part of the group next to ours. 'I heard Andrew asking,' he added as he plonked down on the grass, breathless

'Oh, I have something to eat, but it isn't much,' I said, somewhat apologetically.

'If you have some food, would you mind giving it to the Rabbi?'

I looked up and saw Andrew and Philip standing right in front of me.

I gulped in astonishment, squinting at them, dumbfounded. The Teacher's disciples were actually talking to me! What an honour!

'Well,' Andrew said insistently, 'let's see what you've got.'

I swallowed in embarrassment and held the basket up for his inspection, avoiding eye contact. He peered inside and then passed the basket on to Philip.

'What do you think, Philip?' he asked. 'Will this do?'

Philip glanced sceptically at the basket, then at me, and shrugged nonchalantly. 'A child's picnic,' he said. 'We'll see what the Rabbi has to say.'

'Well, young fellow, what is your name?' Andrew asked, looking directly at me.

'Samuel. His name is Samuel,' Nathan answered for me.

Andrew folded his arms and looked at me very gravely. 'Samuel, will you give your lunch to the Teacher?' he asked kindly.

Speechless, I nodded. My heart was pounding in my chest and

my mouth was dry. My stomach was still rumbling rebelliously, but if Yeshua was hungry and wanted my lunch, how could I possibly refuse him? I considered it an honour and a privilege.

'Right! Come with us, then,' Andrew said, leading the way.

Needless to say, I hastened to obey, almost tripping over in my desire to keep up with him. Nathan and his father followed me, and so did the lad and his friends from the other group. By the time we got to Yeshua we were quite a little band of troopers.

'Master, this boy has some food,' Andrew said, as we approached the Teacher.

Yeshua turned and looked directly at me. I sucked in my breath and so did all the other boys with me. He was even more beautiful than I had imagined, and his brown eyes were gentle and bright. Light seemed to radiate from him. We stared at him in awe.

'What have you got there, my child?' he asked softly.

'Five loaves, two fish and flagon of water,' Andrew answered, sounding very much like the fruit and vegetable venders at the market advertising their wares.

'And you are willing to give it to me?' Yeshua asked kindly.

I nodded wordlessly. I could not speak. My heart was bursting with a love that I had never felt for anyone before. I was trembling with excitement; my legs felt like water, they were so weak and wobbly.

'What is your name, my child?' his soft, tender voice and loving demeanour overwhelmed me.

'Samuel,' I whispered.

'Then I accept your gift with thanks, Samuel,' Yeshua said cheerfully, his eyes sparkling in delight.

MIRACLES

He took the basket I held out to him and opened it. He placed the loaves of bread and fish in the napkin on the boulder he had been sitting on, knelt down with his back to us, opened his arms out in a gesture of prayer, and prayed. Then he got up and told his twelve disciples to start distributing the food to the people.

I could hardly believe my eyes! Suddenly, there were dozens of baskets filled with bread and an equal number to the brim with fish. *Where* did they all come from? They seemed to appear out of thin air!

The disciples quickly distributed the food to the people, but no sooner had they emptied the baskets when more appeared. The people were hungry and devoured the food in a matter of minutes. The disciples were running ragged all over the field hurrying to feed the thousands who had gathered there.

My new friends sat down with Nathan and me to enjoy our lunch. We ate in silence staring in amazement at the hustle and bustle of activity that was swarming all around us.

Mathieu (the boy who had run towards us) was the first to break the silence.

'He performed a similar miracle at my uncle's wedding in Cana,' he said quietly.

'Really?' Nathan's voice was eager with excitement. 'What did he do?'

'He changed water into wine,' Mathieu responded calmly.

There was an audible gasp of astonishment from the little group of children.

'Did you actually *see* it happen?' I was all agog with curiosity.

'Yes,' Mathieu's friend, Rueben, replied. 'Right before our very eyes.'

MIRACLES

'He asked the servants to fill six large jars with water and prayed over them just like he did today,' Mathieu explained. He paused dramatically, looking round the circle at each of us. 'And then, we had wine! Gallons of wine!' He flung his arms wide like a conductor in a concerto at the end of a crescendo.

'It was incredible!' Rueben said, shaking his head in wonder at the memory of it all.

'They say he is the Messiah that the prophets talked about long ago,' Anna, Mathieu's older sister, confided.

'What do *you* think?' Nathan asked her. 'Do *you* think he is the Messiah, too?'

'Yes, I believe he is,' Anna said simply. 'I never saw what happened at the wedding, but Rueben and Mathieu told me all about it. Now I have seen this miracle happen before *my* very eyes, and I believe.'

As we talked, the disciples kept circulating around with huge baskets of bread and fish to serve the people. It was astounding! There seemed to be a never-ending supply of food in baskets that appeared from nowhere. By the end of the afternoon all the people were well fed and satisfied. They talked, laughed and mingled with each other, enjoying themselves as if they were at a wedding. Some of the older folk lay down under the trees and napped. The younger children ran around playing 'Tag', 'Catch Me if You Can' and other games that children love to play, screaming in delight. Everyone seemed to be having a wonderful time. We marvelled at it all and shook our heads in amazement. We had never seen such joy and excitement in our entire lives. It was incredible!

Nathan's father came up to us and told us that we must get going

MIRACLES

if we want to be home before sunset. Reluctantly, we said goodbye to our new friends and cleared up all our things. The disciples were also clearing up the baskets of food and carrying them to the Master. Nathan and I watched as they laid the baskets of leftovers in front of the boulder that Yeshua had been sitting on all the time. There were twelve of them – one for each of the disciples!

My heart raced and my whole body tingled as my hair stood on end. This was no coincidence. We had witnessed something really momentous that day and we were an integral part of it.

As we walked down the hill, my heart was full of joy, peace and the love that Yeshua had shown me when I proffered my picnic basket to him. The memory of his beautiful face as he looked tenderly at me was indelibly etched in my mind, and I hugged it close to my heart for the rest of my life.

MIRACLES

4.
Jesus Heals a Boy

'I'm sorry, Jonathan, there is nothing more I can do for your child,' the doctor said shaking his head sadly as he gathered his instruments together and put them in his bag.

My name is Yosef; I have been ill for as long as I can remember. I would be as right as rain one minute, and down on the floor writhing and foaming the next. Then, just as suddenly as it all began, I would be back to normal again.

My parents could not understand *what* was happening to me, and the doctors could not understand *why*. All they could suggest was to lay me down on the floor whenever I fell, and to make me feel as comfortable as possible. They told my mother to put a smooth wooden stick in between my teeth to stop me from biting my tongue and to take it out as soon as I was better. On a couple of occasions, I even fell into the cooking fire all of a sudden. I sustained severe burns and blisters much to the consternation of my poor overwrought parents. Another time, while crossing the Sea of Galilee, I was thrown into the water without any warning. Fortunately, one of the boatmen was able to swim, and he rescued me.

MIRACLES

I was their only child, so my parents were all the more protective. My mother had slipped and fallen when she was pregnant with me, and she had given birth to me soon afterwards, but unfortunately she could not have any more children. I was fine for the first few years of my life, but the problems started seven years ago just after my fifth birthday. My parents tried everything they could think of, but to no avail. Doctors would come and go and they would all say the same thing. It was absolutely hopeless.

That day, our servant, Saul, told my father that the Rabbi was coming to town and that he should take me to the city centre to ask him to heal me.

We were from Bethsaida, which is a city on the east bank of the River Jordan, near where the estuary enters the Sea of Tiberias, or as it is popularly known, the Sea of Galilee. Surrounding the city were vast wastelands and deserts, beyond which towered the majestic Mount Tabor, just north of Caesarea Philippi.

We had heard amazing stories about wonderful healings and deliverances done by the Master that were nothing short of miraculous. People said such lovely things about the brilliant young man called Yeshua, who was a carpenter from Nazareth, and my parents thought that it would be a good idea to follow their servant's lead. It would take us to where we were meant to go. So we all set out for Bethsaida straightaway.

When we reached the city, a huge crowd had gathered there. We hurried along hoping that we would not miss our chance of a miracle. Our servant, Saul, recognised some of the Rabbi's disciples, but as we drew nearer to them, we could see no sign of the Rabbi himself. My father and Saul spoke to one of the disciples.

'Where is your Master?' my father asked.

The disciple, who turned out to be Andrew, shrugged his shoulders and spread his hands out in a nonchalant gesture of ignorance. 'I don't know,' he said. 'Is there anything we can help you with, sir?'

'Yes,' my father replied. 'My son is ill. We were hoping that the Rabbi would heal him.'

Andrew turned round and looked at me. Then he called out to Philip and asked him to come over.

Philip sprinted over at once. 'What is the matter, Andrew?' he asked.

Andrew whispered something to Philip, who nodded. Then Andrew turned back to my father, laid a comforting hand on his shoulder and said reassuringly, 'We will see what we can do, sir. Have faith.'

Then Andrew attracted the attention of the other disciples, who came over and formed a circle around me. Andrew stepped into the middle with me and began to call out the evil spirit from me in a loud voice, to no avail. Then Philip took over, but still nothing happened. I just stood there, inert, staring into space.

The disciples gathered together to have a discussion on how they should proceed, as they agreed that they were going nowhere. They whispered among themselves and I noticed some of them nodding vehemently in agreement to what Andrew was saying. My parents looked at each other and at Saul in despair. My mother's eyes were wide with fear; she was as pale as a ghost. My father was wringing his hands in desperation.

After a few minutes, the disciples returned and this time they formed a semicircle in front of me. Then, they all started calling out the evil spirit in unison; yet, the louder they called, the more aggressive the spirit got, and I fell on the floor shaking violently.

By this time, a large crowd had gathered around the disciples and people started speculating on what was going on.

'These are the Rabbi's disciples,' said one, who looked suspiciously like a Pharisee. 'What are they trying to do with this poor child?' The disapproval in his voice could not be mistaken.

'I think they are trying to emulate their Master,' replied his younger companion sarcastically.

'They are not doing a very good job of it!' snorted the Pharisee indignantly. 'If they are not careful they will injure the boy at best, and kill him at worst! They should not be allowed to do this. Where *is* the Rabbi?'

'We have done this before, you know,' said Philip who had been standing a little outside the semicircle. 'And with great success, if I might add,' he went on with a confident smile. 'Some of them take a bit of time to cooperate.'

'Cooperate! Humbug!' spluttered the older Pharisee, who was not in the least bit impressed, and by now had started to hyperventilate. He glared belligerently at Philip. He had literally turned quite red in the face and seemed in danger of bursting a blood vessel!

The disciples tried to order the evil spirit out of me by shouting louder and louder, but without results. Then suddenly, someone shouted to us that the Master was coming back down the mountain.

Some people ran up to him as he reached the foot of Mount Tabor, and immediately reported to him what was happening.

MIRACLES

'Master, your disciples are trying to cast out the evil spirit from this boy, but nothing is happening. They don't have your power, my Lord,' one of the men said.

'They are going to kill him!' cried another. 'He keeps falling down and banging his head on the ground.'

'His mother is very distressed, Master. She is crying. Please help her,' implored another.

Yeshua and the three disciples, Peter, James and John, who had gone with him up the mountain, hurried through the crowd that parted voluntarily to let them through. When my father saw Yeshua, he rushed towards him and fell at his feet.

'Teacher,' my father cried. 'I brought you my son, who is possessed by a spirit that has robbed him of speech. Whenever it seizes him it throws him to the ground. He foams at the mouth, gnashes his teeth and becomes rigid. I asked your disciples to drive out the spirit, but they could not do it.'

Yeshua was looking down at him with so much love, compassion and understanding in his beautiful, expressive brown eyes that my father could not bear it. He started to weep uncontrollably. My mother stepped forward to comfort him and they both knelt there in front of the Lord, and wept.

Yeshua glared angrily around at the crowd and the Pharisees, until his eyes rested on his disciples who were shamefacedly avoiding his gaze.

'You unbelieving generation!' he cried, his eyes blazing with fire. 'How long shall I put up with you? Bring the boy to me.' He spoke with so much authority that the clamouring crowd was silenced. You could have heard a pin drop.

MIRACLES

So the disciples brought me to Yeshua. When the spirit saw Yeshua, it immediately threw me into a convulsion. I fell to the ground, rolling around and foaming at the mouth.

Then Yeshua asked my father, 'How long has he been like this?'

'From childhood,' my father replied, sobbing pitifully. 'It has often thrown him into the fire or water to kill him.' He clasped his hands under his chin and looked up at Yeshua through his tears. 'Master, if you can do anything, take pity on us and help us,' he beseeched.

'*If you can?*' Yeshua asked. 'Everything is possible for the one who believes.'

Immediately my father exclaimed, 'I *do* believe, help me overcome my unbelief.'

Then Yeshua rebuked the unclean spirit. 'You deaf and mute spirit,' he said sternly, 'I command you to come out of him and never enter him again.'

The spirit shrieked, convulsed me violently again, and came out. I lay on the floor motionless and as pale as a corpse. Several people in the crowd around me whispered in horror, 'He's dead!' But Yeshua crouched down beside me; he took me by the hands, lifted me to my feet, and I stood up. I stared at him as if seeing him for the first time. I felt as if a weight had been lifted off me. I experienced an overwhelming surge of peace and joy engulf me. His eyes met mine and I could see love and tenderness flow out of them to me. He smiled sweetly at me and I smiled back at him. Then with childlike trust, I reached out my arms to him and hugged him. He laughed and held me close to him for a brief moment, and time stood still. I will remember that moment for the rest of my life as I vowed that I would

MIRACLES

spend it following him.

He turned to my parents and with his arms still around me, grinning broadly, he said, 'I give you back your son. Go in peace.'

The floodgates of gratitude overflowed from my parents' hearts too, and they fell at his feet, still sobbing, but now with joy. They both reached out their arms to me and gathered me in a warm embrace holding me close for a long time as if they would never let me go.

5.
The Syro-Phoenician Girl

My first impression of the ancient city of Jerusalem was that it was the most elegant historical city in the Middle East. Nestled among majestic mountains, verdant olive groves and beautiful gardens, it was, to my mind, the most picturesque city that I had ever had the pleasure to live in.

My name is Tanit and I am 15 years old. I am going to tell you how I came to live in the Holy City of Jerusalem five years ago.

One day, I woke up to the sounds of yelling. I sighed in resignation: my parents, I thought. They were always arguing. Over me. Not a single day passed by when they didn't have a shouting match, and I was always the reason. My health, my problems, my welfare.

Of course, my parents only had my best interests at heart. I never doubted that. They wanted me to get well – run around and play like all the other children did, but I could not. I was constantly suffering from terrible headaches and could hardly speak a word. I was only 4

MIRACLES

years old. I remember the problems started when I took a fall from the bed a couple of years earlier. I had hit my head on the floor as I toppled forwards onto it. After that I suffered from blurred vision and intense headaches, more than I could bear. I would cry bitterly when they came about and my mother would cry along with me. My father would shout and leave the house in anger. He blamed her for my infirmities.

I sat up in bed and watched them battling with each other for some time.

'This would never have happened if you hadn't left her alone with the maid in the first place,' my father shouted.

'I know and I am *sorry*,' my mother sobbed. 'How many times do I have to tell you that?'

'For the rest of our lives, I suppose,' my father retorted angrily.

'Will you never forgive me for that?' my mother pleaded pitifully.

My father turned away. 'I'm going to work. I've had enough of this for one day,' he barked, flinging his arm over his head in frustration.

I climbed out of bed and padded to my mother. 'Mama,' I cried, stretching out my arms towards her in a non-verbal request to be carried. The only words I ever uttered were 'Mama' and my nurse's name, 'Anna'. I did not have any kind of relationship with my father because he ignored me completely.

'Tanit, you are awake!' my mother exclaimed. She immediately scooped me up in her arms and called to my nurse to bring me some milk.

'The Rabbi is in town, my lady,' said Anna quietly as she handed my mother a cup of milk. 'He will be able to heal Tanit if you ask him.'

MIRACLES

MIRACLES

'Aha!' my mother responded excitedly. 'Do you know where I might find him?' she asked.

'I believe he is staying with your friends Hurum and Hannah, my lady,' my nurse replied.

I drank the milk as my mother tidied up my hair, gently rocking me in her arms.

'I will go there at once,' she said decisively. 'I have heard a lot about the Rabbi from Hannah. He changed water into wine at her sister's wedding. I believe in him.'

'Shall I come with you, my lady?' Anna asked hopefully. She wanted to see the Rabbi too. Though she was Jewish she had never seen him.

'No!' My mother's response was prompt. She had made up her mind to go in search of the Rabbi to beg him to heal me. 'You must stay here and look after Tanit. I will go with Hadad. Tell him to get the chariot ready now.'

After a confrontation with the Pharisees in Jerusalem, Jesus and his disciples travelled north-west to the region of Tyre and Sidon. They were very tired after their long journey, and went into the house of Hurum and Hannah where they were scheduled to stay for a few days. After a filling and nourishing meal they retired to rest for a while, as it was very hot and they needed a time of refreshing.

Unfortunately for them, their time of relaxation was short-lived as my mother burst into the house unannounced and demanded to see the Rabbi. The servants were terrified and scurried off to call their mistress, who hurried to find out what was happening.

'Oh, Resheph, it's you,' she said, a little breathless with embarrassment. Obviously, the servants had told her why my mother had come.

'Hannah, I need to see the Rabbi,' my mother said imperiously. 'I want him to heal my daughter.'

'He is resting right now. He is very tired.' Hannah appeared flustered. 'Would you like some refreshment while you wait for him?' she asked placatingly.

'No! I do not!' my mother expostulated quite rudely. 'I must see him at once. I want him to heal Tanit. I know he can.'

While she was still speaking, the Master emerged from one of the adjoining rooms.

'I heard raised voices and woke up,' he said. 'What is the problem?'

Some of his disciples followed him from the interior of the house at the sound of all the commotion and stood beside him as if guarding him from harm.

'We did not mean to wake you, Rabbi.' Hannah was most apologetic.

'Lord, Son of David, have mercy on me!' my mother cried pathetically. 'My daughter is demon-possessed and suffering terribly.'

Jesus did not say a word. He just looked at her gently and tenderly. She stared back at him and broke down weeping. He was not at all as she had expected – so young, so beautiful and so kind. She felt her heart melt within her.

'Send her away, Master,' Jesus' disciples urged him, rubbing the sleep from their eyes. 'She is disturbing our rest and causing a lot of trouble.'

MIRACLES

MIRACLES

Then Jesus answered, 'I was sent only to the lost sheep of Israel.'

Undeterred, my mother came and knelt before him. 'Lord, help me!' she cried desperately.

Yeshua did not take his eyes off her as he calmly looked down at her. 'It is not right to take the children's bread and toss it to the dogs,' he replied.

'Yes, it is, Lord,' my mother persisted doggedly. 'Even the dogs eat the crumbs that fall from their master's table.'

Yeshua's disciples gasped in astonishment and Hannah too drew in her breath sharply. The Master, however, looked round at them all triumphantly.

Then he said to my mother, 'Woman, you have great faith! Your request is granted.'

My mother stretched her arms on the floor and worshiped at his feet, tears streaming down her face. 'Thank you! Thank you so much!' She was overcome with gratitude now.

She returned to her chariot and they drove like the wind. As soon as she got home, she jumped out of the carriage and ran into the house. 'Tanit! Tanit, where are you?' she called.

Hearing her voice, I ran to her and jumped into her arms. 'I am here, Mother,' I said.

She looked at me and held me close to her heart, burying her face in my long curly hair, sobbing uncontrollably.

'She has been delivered and healed,' Anna said joyfully.

'When did this happen?' my mother asked her.

'About half an hour ago,' Anna replied.

'Aha!' my mother exclaimed. 'That was the time the Lord told me

MIRACLES

that my daughter was healed. How extraordinary!'

Anna was smiling from ear to ear. 'I told you he would heal her, didn't I, my lady?'

'Yes, you did,' my mother said, also smiling happily, bobbing me up and down in her arms. 'Yes, Anna, indeed you did! Thank you!'

When my father came home late that evening and saw that I was well, he asked my mother what had happened. My mother told him about her meeting with the Rabbi. He gazed at her admiringly and gathered us both into a warm embrace.

We were a family again.

The Rabbi certainly was an extraordinary person and he made wonderful things happen. So that is why, as followers of Yeshua, we came to live in the beautiful city of Jerusalem.

Epilogue

The Jesus of the Bible (Yeshua) is not just a Miracle Worker or a great Teacher. He is the Son of God, who came down to earth and died on the Cross for the sins of the whole world. Through His death, burial and resurrection, He obtained salvation for us. He is now alive in Heaven in glory, and will soon come back again to take all those who believe in Him, to be with Him forever.

You can have an assurance of Heaven by putting your faith in what Jesus did on the Cross for you. Just say a simple prayer from your heart and put your trust in Jesus, as the only way of salvation is through Him. That being done, you will come into a Covenant relationship with the God of the Universe. Imagine how awesome that will be!

God bless you!
Shalom, shalom!

Bibliography – The Holy Bible (NIV)

1. The Wedding Feast at Cana John 2:1-10

2. Jairus's Daughter   Luke 8:45-56

3. Five Loaves and Two Fish   John 6:8-13

4. Jesus Heals a Boy   Mark 9:14-29

5. The Syro-Phoenician Girl   Mark 7:24-30